THANKS FOR WAITING
Issue n° 15 — Autumn 2020

MW00788829

PART 1

Beaches, books and juniper berries: this season's cover star
SARAH JESSICA PARKER is photographed by Roe Ethridge
in Amagansett, Long Island.

PART 2

Our Book of the Season, JAPANESE GHOST STORIES,
is centre of gravity to a series of hallucinatory artworks;
correspondents around the world compile an obsessive yet
fragmentary portrait of the book's odd author, Lafcadio Hearn.

This issue's endpaper pattern is based on the
Japanese printmaking technique *bokashi*. During
the Edo period (1603–1868), *bokashi* was used to
create the beautiful colour gradations in *ukiyo-e*
woodcut art

A reader absorbed, beneath Singer, Kafka and Neruda, in the American bookshop Barnes & Noble. Photograph by IAN BERRY.

TO BE SEEN

The trouble with ebooks is that no one else can see what you're reading. Like it or not, books are an astonishingly efficient accessory. A Woolf, an Ellison, a Sappho, an Ishiguro, a Gallant or a Perec — carried with insouciant familiarity, a book by these or any writer of note, except perhaps Rand, outguns a neck chain, a handbag, an anklet or a Rolex. That's just the way it is. The unparalleled decorative power of book jackets is one of the twelve great reasons why print will persist.

The rise of the spectated video call has brought these qualities out of hiding. Nobody serious would agree to do an interview from home with the BBC without a few bound paper things in the background. These were scrutinized and discussed in *New York Times* features and dedicated 'shelves of the famous' social media accounts, and of course caught the attention of *The Happy Reader*. It's how we learned that the actor Tom Hanks has all three volumes of *The Presidential Recordings of Lyndon Johnson*, containing nearly 800 hours of phone transcripts pertaining to governmental business. Or that wellness magnate Gwyneth Paltrow has a coffee table book about the rich and famous people who lived in the French Riviera in the '20s and '30s. Or that cellist Yo-Yo Ma has *With Your Own Two Hands*, a book about overcoming stage fright. Or that Prince Charles has a biography of the eighteenth-century horse painter Basil Taylor.

Perhaps all this talk of accessories and decoration seems shallow. It doesn't have to be. Book ostentation is not only about projecting — or faking — a deeper facet of one's personality than is available with a denim jacket or porcelain rabbit. It's also idealistic. To love a book is to be overcome by an innate desire to advertise it, so that others might read it and love it too. When there's a book we've enjoyed but can't keep, and we leave it on the communal wall, and then we come back later and it's gone, it's fulfilling in a shimmeringly complex way. Someone else might be reading it: someone else's mind might be becoming just that little bit more connected to our own.

THE HAPPY READER
Bookish Magazine
Issue n° 15 — Autumn 2020

The Happy Reader is
a collaboration between
Penguin Books and
Fantastic Man

EDITOR-IN-CHIEF
Seb Emina

MANAGING EDITOR
Maria Bedford

ART DIRECTOR
Tom Etherington

EDITORIAL DIRECTORS
Jop van Bennekom
Gert Jonkers

PICTURE RESEARCH
Frances Roper

PRODUCTION
Katy Banyard

DESIGN CONCEPT
Jop van Bennekom
Helios Capdevila

BRAND DIRECTOR
Sam Voulters

MARKETING DIRECTOR
Ingrid Matts

PUBLISHER
Stefan McGrath

CONTRIBUTORS
Travis Elborough, Roe Ethridge,
Paul Flynn, Moeko Fujii, Jordan
Kelly, Bess Lovejoy, John Self,
Lieko Shiga

THANK YOU
Magnus Åkesson, Richard
Duguid, Michael Famighetti,
Ann Friedman, Samantha
Johnson, Olga Kominek,
Katherine McCulloch, Serge
Normant, Jay Osman, Liz
Parsons, Aaron Peck, Nina Perry,
Three Lives & Company

Penguin Books
80 Strand
London WC2R 0RL

info@thehappyreader.com
www.thehappyreader.com

SNIPPETS

That essential noticeboard for news, gossip and bookish miscellany.

MATERIAL — The Noname Book Club is the most prominent of a new wave of reading groups focusing on books by authors of colour. Now with more than 10,000 members, the club, which was founded last year by US rapper Noname, takes place both online and via real-world events organised by local chapters. It assigns two books per month, which have so far included works by authors Toni Morrison, Brit Bennett, Frantz Fanon and Audre Lorde.

GROWER — An entire forest exists in Norway that was planted for the purpose of supplying paper for just one book: an anthology entitled *Future Library*. A different famous writer (Margaret Atwood is one) is chosen every year to contribute. These contributions are then sealed away until a different lifetime, the plan being that no reader will see them until the book is published in 2114, a hundred years after the forest was planted.

PAL — During a train journey, so as to decide which passages to read at an upcoming talk, the British author Christie Watson was looking through a copy of her own book, when an unknown man in the seat opposite leaned forward and said: 'I know the author. She's a friend.'

SEASONAL — *The Fifth Season*, the new album by French-Iranian-Egyptian musician Lafawndah, takes a title and much inspiration from the Broken Earth trilogy by science fiction author N. K. Jemisin. For those who haven't been glued to them: the books are set on a planet with a single supercontinent called the Stillness, the eponymous 'fifth season' being that of catastrophic climate change.

BASED — Here's a round-up of clunkingly massive movie adaptations with frustratingly vague release dates: Baz Luhrmann is directing a film of Mikhail Bulgakov's novel *The Master and Margarita*; Spike Lee is working on a hip-hop adaptation of *Romeo & Juliet* (it's called *Prince of Cats*); Pedro Almodóvar is taking on Lucia Berlin's story collection *A Manual for Cleaning Women*; Maggie Gyllenhaal will make her directorial debut with a movie of Elena Ferrante's *The Lost Daughter*.

PIVOT — Author Robin Sloan, known for novels including *Mr. Penumbra's 24-Hour Bookstore*, has a brand of olive oil called Fat Gold.

EDITION — A writer offers a service whereby he writes a book from scratch, on demand, in an edition of strictly one. Jason Stoneking, an American in Paris, offers three tiers of output, varying from twenty (hand-written) pages to two hundred, and gives clients the option of speaking to him about the 'themes that they're wrestling with' before he begins to write.

LEAK FLAN — There is no more quintessentially twenty-first-century cookbook than *Leaked Recipes*, consisting as it does of cookery techniques, including those for 'overnight oatmeal' and 'crabmeat imperial', that its author, Demetria Gladstone, unearthed in major tranches of leaked emails.

OLD BATH — It is possible to rent one of Jane Austen's former houses on Airbnb. The two-bedroom property is in Bath, Somerset, where the Austen family lived from 1801 to 1805. Jane would later use the spa city as a setting in both *Northanger Abbey* and *Persuasion*. The house, which has (alas?) been redecorated quite a few times since then, has a 4.95 star average from 148 reviews.

SARAH JESSICA PARKER

In conversation with PAUL FLYNN
Portraits by ROE ETHRIDGE

Oh yes, kick off the Sunday shoes! Sarah Jessica Parker is and always will be associated with *Sex and the City*, that beacon of late 90s Manhattanism and a voguish binge-watch to this day, but there's so much more to her than the zingy wisdom of sex columnist Carrie Bradshaw. SJP's non-*SATC* roles encompass movies *Footloose* and *The Family Stone*, TV shows *Glee* and *Divorce*, and a Broadway show (now rescheduled for spring) with husband Matthew Broderick, not to mention a parade of offscreen projects such as a clothing line, a perfume brand, and a publishing imprint, SJP for Hogarth.

Sarah Jessica Parker, 55, is a prolific and wide-ranging reader too, and that's what propels this romping page-turner of a lock-down interview.

MANHATTAN

Sarah Jessica Parker was deep into a tech run for the first preview of Neil Simon's *Plaza Suite* when Governor Andrew Cuomo and Mayor Bill DeBlasio shut down Broadway. It was Thursday, 12 March. Curtain up at the Hudson Theatre was due at 7.30pm, yet the atmosphere that afternoon was noticeably strange. 'We were about to do our first public performance that night,' she says on the telephone from New York, where she is isolating with her family. 'And at five o'clock Broadway closed.'

Plaza Suite was a project of particular personal significance for the actor. She was starring in the two-hander against her husband, Matthew Broderick, the first time they'd performed together in twenty-three years of partnership. When they began dating, Parker and Broderick spent hours unfolding the similarities in their back stories. Their return to Broadway should've been a crowning glory, one of Manhattan's democratically championed Prom Kings and Queens arriving back for coronation.

Our first conversation lasts two hours. It takes place on 5 May, seven weeks into lockdown. Outside, the barely discernible, ghostly echoes of silenced metropolitan chaos (New York her end, London mine) frame the conversation. Yet the momentum of Sarah Jessica Parker's warm, thoughtful storytelling capacity never dips. Her voice is so familiar I spend the first ten minutes teaching myself a quick mental reflex mechanism to extract us from an imaginary episode of *Sex and the City*.

Sarah Jessica Parker is not just a storyteller by trade. She has her own imprint at the esteemed publisher Crown, and is patron of the New York Public Library. When she scaled the dizziest heights of fame between 1998 and 2004, she did so by playing a writer. Carrie Bradshaw was extracted from a real-life author and magazine veteran, Candace Bushnell.

Sex and the City was a special fantasia of what a writer's life might look like, making Carrie Bradshaw both composite of and inspiration for a generation of magazine writers. She reversed the gender balance in television's sex games, punctuating them with weekly written missives on modern love that made her an Inspector Columbo or Miss

Marple of the heart. 'People still believe I am Carrie Bradshaw,' she will say at one point during our conversations. That is some sleight of hand for an actor to pull off.

Sarah Jessica Parker brought women to the elite TV network HBO in droves. When she returned to the network in the sobering break-up black comedy *Divorce* (2016), she did so first with the help of another brilliant relationship diarist, Sharon Horgan. By then, the Carrie Bradshaw writer-as-protagonist model had become a staple of 21st century TV. They were everywhere.

The actor's great love of storytelling is directly connected to her understanding of the power of words. At the time of writing, *Plaza Suite* has been shelved for a year. Mr and Mrs Sarah Jessica Parker will have to wait until March 2021 to step back on stage, into more innocent times.

PAUL FLYNN: How does New York look today?

SARAH JESSICA PARKER: It's all so unfamiliar, and that does play peculiar games with your brain. What are days and what are weekends? How to be productive? What does that even mean when most of the activity toward productivity is work-related? How much of that is undoable? And then kids and the larger, devastating headline picture of what you know is happening. It is just crushing. You're at sixes and sevens what to do, how to be helpful, where to focus your energies and your dollars. Who needs help the most? What is urgent? It's unimaginable.

P: On a personal level, have you had a temptation to compare what's happening in your life in real time to the life you should've been living on Broadway right now? This was supposed to be a crowning moment for you, surely?

S: Well, I don't know that we would categorise it as a crowning moment. But we were supposed to be working. We had just finished in Boston and we had come into New York. I think back to that time and I can't tell myself what I knew then. My husband and I had gotten very sick in Boston. Unusually sick. We had to cancel a show, then I missed a show and we came to New York and it existed, this idea of something looming. I try to recall what I actually knew, what I understood it to be, what we didn't know, how we were all behaving. Feeling slightly embarrassed about our reticence to be physical with each other. Bumping elbows. Apologizing, 'Sorry, I'm not going to hug you.'

P: Did the timing of lockdown feel particularly merciless for you?

S: What we were going to do that night was the traditional thing you do on Broadway, which was a first preview. We were running the

Parker's weekend house is in Amagansett, a hamlet in The Hamptons, Long Island.

show on stage, but it felt unglued. There was so much quiet activity in the house, which is not typical. We had stopped to fix a light cue and I kept seeing people whispering. Now I can't remember what we thought was coming. But I guess I was waiting for the truth, which was that the governor was going to shut down Broadway, for all the right reasons. So yeah, we would've been up and running. I'm missing where we should've been. I miss working. I miss that experience we fought so long and hard for. But what are you going to do? There are larger problems, people are suffering and I'm not suggesting that ours compares to the health and economic devastation that is rampant.

P: What had the Boston run of the play taught you?

S: We had strong suspicions that Neil Simon, who hadn't been produced a lot lately, could still connect. Before you put it in front of an audience, that speculation is hope. Even though it is a vintage piece — in some ways a relic because it really speaks of a different time, especially in terms of the role women play in marriages, work and sexual politics — it played beautifully. What we learned is that the play works. It was timely in its innocence.

P: How do you think reading scripts at such a young age informed your adult taste for literature?

S: Gosh, I've never thought about that. I guess what I always liked when I read scripts, which is the same experience I have now as a reader for pleasure, is what is unfamiliar. What haven't I done? The more opportunities that I had to read scripts, the more I was interested in what was new and unfamiliar. That's the kind of reader I am today, in large part because of my mom. She always wanted to be someone else growing up, outside her home, outside her school, outside her social circle that maybe she didn't feel part of. She had such curiosity and wanderlust which she never really got to fulfil. I think books transported her. She forced us to be readers at a very young age. We didn't have a television, just books and a record player.

P: Back when you started the Crown imprint, what was the one New York shop you wanted to be stocked in? What's your iconic New York bookstore?

S: For those of us from Lower Manhattan, the store that we all gravitate to, the beating heart of the West Village, is Three Lives, a really special bookstore on West 4th and Waverley. The owner's name is Toby, and it's an absolutely exquisite shop. It's physically beautiful, an old building painted in a high-gloss bright red on the outside. Every nook and cranny is filled with books. The sales associates are very learned, devoted readers. They always leave a note that says, 'oh

1. NEIL SIMON

—

The great Broadway playwright, who died in 2018, was a master of poignant domestic comedy. The secret ingredient, as he saw it, was the concoction of difficult choices. '*Dilemma* is the key word,' he said. 'It is always a dilemma, not a situation.'

2. THE FAMILY STONE
—
Parker as Meredith Morton, a socially-cold executive, struggling to fit in with her boyfriend's family at Christmas, in comedy-drama film *The Family Stone* (2005).

Troy loves this book,' or, 'This is Joyce's favourite all year.' And if Troy or Joyce have loved that book, that is a very encouraging sign. Three Lives is central to all of our lives in the West Village. You can say that name to anybody within a twenty-block radius.

P: What's the great New York novel?

S: Oh my god. There's a few. Let's see. From a young person, before I lived in New York, there was a young adult book called *The Mixed up Files of Mrs Basil E Frankweiler*. Do you know it?

P: No, tell.

S: It's a book about two young kids from Greenwich, Connecticut, a young girl, somewhere between 11 and 13, who perceives some terrible injustice in her house, as young teenagers do, and plans to run away. She has two siblings, brothers I believe. The youngest boy is very miserly, frugal and spends none of his earned money. He's got quite the nest egg. So, she cleverly chooses him to accompany her. They run away, take the Metro north from Greenwich to New York City and move into the Metropolitan Museum of Art. It's just spectacular. I tried to force it on my daughters when they were seven and they could barely read and they were just, like, Mama, we don't understand a word of what you are talking about. Finally, their faces had morphed into question marks. That's my first New York book. The director of *The Family Stone* gave me, oh, what is the book?

P: I adore *The Family Stone*. It's in my top three Christmas movies ever.

S: Oh, thank you. I loved making that movie. That was a really lovely experience. And that director is a guy named Tom [Bezucha], who gave me *Winter's Tale* by Mark Halperin. Again, its fantastical but I absolutely loved that book. Silly as it sounds, there's a great book that was introduced to me by my husband when we were courting, called *Time and Again*, a novel by Jack Finney. It is fiction but based on time and events in New York at the turn of the century and it's beautifully researched. Mixed among this perfectly researched story is a sweeping romance. It's a beloved book and it's a time machine. There is actually a time machine in the book, if you believe in those things. And boy, do I wish I had one now.

P: Do you think a book that you're given by someone at the start of an enduring love casts a shadow over what that relationship becomes?

S: Absolutely, yes. It's like scar tissue. You build up a whole thing around all those shared experiences. Restaurants, books, records, movies are all part of that courtship. You pounce on it as some kind of foundation later. I would not have known about that book had

Matthew not told me about it. Let's do a recent [New York] book. James McBride's *Deacon King Kong* is absolutely a New York story, about a housing project in Brooklyn. It's about class, politics, religion, racism and people who are reliant on government assistance and what that does, how it traps people. It's a beautiful story. I think it's an important book. The scope is big and tiny, like all great books. I posted that book and people on Instagram will tell me things I didn't know about him.

P: Books are a safe social media space.
 S: It only sparks kindness, excitement and enthusiasm if I post about a book. They're the least controversial thing I can talk about on Instagram. You could go for days without someone saying something snarky, rude, scary, mean, political or bitter.

P: Is enveloping yourself in a book an intense or a relief experience for you?
 S: Well, sometimes I think I read too fast. My husband reads very slowly and remembers every detail. I don't know whether you've ever had this when you're reading a book, that you have a stomach-ache by trying to slow yourself down? It's unique to that feeling of urgency about a book. Also, often I will do anything to not finish a book. And I never read a book twice. I don't see any point in it. What book do you read over and over? None!

P: I started re-reading, as I became middle-aged, the books that had meant a lot to me, particularly as a teenager, as a sort of test of my life experience.
 S: I will do that. Case in point: Salinger. I re-read *Franny and Zooey* and *Raise High the Roof Beam, Carpenters*. The *Nine Stories*. It is all about who you thought you were and your response to the book and where you are in your life now. Some of that stuff I was like, how did I ever get through this? *Raise High the Roof* is really dense and super hard to read.

P: One book I would absolutely consider to be a great New York novel is Tama Janovitz's *Slaves of New York*.
 S: My god, I haven't read that in years, definitely since it came out.

P: That's one on my revisit pile. It was the book that made me fall hook, line and sinker in love with the idea of New York as a teenager.
 S: People say the same about Patti Smith's book.

P: Another outsider classic.

3. INSTAGRAM
—
At the time of writing Sarah Jessica Parker's Instagram account (her name all one word) has 6.2 million followers and follows 369 accounts including comedian Sarah Cooper, fashion journalist André Leon Talley, and 'Curb Alert NYC', whose mission is to reduce landfill by sharing reusable items found on the streets of NYC.

S: I'm so embarrassed I haven't read it, but everybody says that it is the perfect New York book. I'm going to put that on the top of the list.

P: What is it that makes New York such a city of letters? Is it the volume of the city, voices trying to stick their hands in the air to be heard above the rabble?

S: I don't know. I wonder. There was a period that I was worried that New York, Manhattan in particular, even some of the outer boroughs, have become just so prohibitive for artists. Who can live in the city? Where is all the art going to come from that speaks of their time and this, their home. The art that is going to come now may not be born of Manhattan but those who reside downstate. Can you imagine the writing that's happening right now? In solitary. What will emerge? My guess is that those voices are saying, I want to be seen and I want to be heard and the only way I can do it in such a loud place is to put the most quiet thing, which is the most startling and can draw the most attention onto paper and let the words speak on a page. With books, you don't have to scream to be heard. It's the most eloquent way of screaming.

P: The conversation is so lyrical in the city. There's such a unique vernacular shared by New Yorkers.

S: would think that about London, too. Good lord, talk about a city of letters.

P: Don't flip it back. Your most famous role is as an absolute embodiment of those rhythmic New York speech patterns. Carrie Bradshaw was a figurehead of the wise-cracking, knowing, cynical, whip-smart one liner that is utterly unique to the city.

S: [a little shyly] I guess that is uniquely New York.

P: Candace Bushnell felt to me like an upscale Tama Janovitz, ten years later.

S: Oh, definitely.

P: Was it weird to become that famous playing a writer?

S: Yes! That book was sent to me anonymously, and I don't mean in a scary way. I don't remember why it was sent to me. But I knew of her columns in the *New York Observer*. I had read a lot of them. I knew the minute I started reading them that she was definitely a fresh, smart, very much new and singular voice. I read it and I was wowed by her, as everybody was. If you meet Candace in person, it's even better. She can really hold court. She is a fast, funny and very,

4. VERNACULAR
—
For example 'stoop' meaning 'steps at front of building', 'brick' meaning 'incredibly cold', and 'regular coffee' meaning 'coffee with absurd amounts of cream and sugar'.

5. CANDACE BUSHNELL
—
The premise, name and heroine of *Sex and the City* originated in Bushnell's mid-1990s dating column for the *New York Observer*. Last year Bushnell published a book entitled *Is There Still Sex in the City?*, about 'the wilds and lows of sex and dating after fifty'.

very good storyteller. She's a sparkling person to be around, and I wasn't surprised to see her have that success. The thing about playing a writer was that I was always trying to pay attention to language choices. Michael Patrick [King] and I would work so closely initially with Darren Starr, who created the show. I felt like I had to be a gatekeeper of language. I would say, but she's a writer, she can't be lazy about that, she has to love words and love language and she can't just use foul language and be salty and ribald just because we're on HBO. It wasn't a constant problem, but I didn't want her to use the f-word all the time. If she used it, I wanted it to be very thoughtful and have some impact. I loved that Carrie was a writer and she loved being a writer. Her professional life was enormously important to her. The one thing I cared most about was how she chose to communicate, how articulate and verbal she can be. Not to be show-offy but because she would be reaching out for a hand-in-glove relationship with words.

P: Was Candace herself intimidating when you first met her?

S: She wasn't. She was very different from me and she wasn't involved in the show, she wasn't part of the writing staff. I met her socially a little bit when we first started. Darren would put dinners together. I was delighted by her. She was much braver and much more outgoing than I had ever been and … am. She was much more confident socially, a natural central focus of gatherings, and that suited her. So, it wasn't intimidating, but it was impressive. I didn't feel that I had to be Candace. By the time Darren had worked the story up, she wasn't Candace, but it was very helpful to see somebody who had spent those years in that life. Because I hadn't. I liked her bravado and courage and her intimacy with the night-time in the city. My night-time would be going to work on stage or on a film set and then maybe to Centrale, having dinner with people, then going home.

P: Do you think about the influence Carrie had in terms of people wanting to become writers? I've worked on a lot of women's magazines since *Sex and the City* started and I can guarantee you that most of the writers have, at one point or another had to stop themselves writing '… and then I got to thinking'. I know I've done it.

S: That's amazing. I have people stop me on the street all the time and say, 'I am here, I am in New York because of Carrie Bradshaw.' Not just women, men too. I can't tell you if that is hundreds or thousands now. I lost count. They say, 'I came to New York because I want to be a writer like Carrie.' But really, that's to be a writer like Candace. That's her story that became Carrie's. I still get it. It's very touching that she created a character and Darren then made his own version and Michael took very good care of this character that was so flawed — I mean, so many people objected to her profligacy and the way she chose to spend her disposable income — but I think she was a decent, loyal friend. And she was a devoted professional.

P: She was utterly fabulous. When we think about the way HBO turned the flashlight from exterior storytelling on TV into the interior lives of its protagonists, she is just as vital as Tony Soprano. But when we talk about Tony Soprano now, we don't talk about his mass organised crime. We talk about his messed-up psychology, his trying to be a better man. When we talk about Carrie Bradshaw, we talk about her shoe shopping.
    S: Ab...so...lutely. Look, you are far more generous than some of your colleagues. I would always say, it's so curious to me that Tony Soprano was a murderer, but you don't ever ask the actor about that. Then I would get, how do you feel about playing someone who sleeps around, drinks, is so unlikeable and spends so much money on shoes? It's so curious to me that they don't ask our beloved, missed actor James how he felt playing a murderer. It was always, he's so interesting, he's so complicated.

P: Was Carrie Bradshaw the last fanfare of an archetype of print journalism who no longer exists?
    S: It does speak of that very specific time, in a way specific to Condé Nast and the empire that it was. Even when I'm with hairdressers, makeup-artists and stylists, they still talk about it, because they were on the receiving end of it, too. The kind of lives, the salaries, the dinners at restaurants in Paris, Milan, London, the expense accounts. It's just hard to imagine that it existed. Also, they were not alone in that corporate culture.

P: The fashion in the show stands up so well. I was looking at some episodes recently and it's all Prada square-toed heels and Dior saddle bags. It's totally 2020.
    S: That's so funny. That's all Pat [Field]. She's otherworldly.

P: She was a storyteller with fashion in a way that was every bit the equal of those scripts.
    S: Absolutely. Costume design isn't often talked about, but it's integral, it's crucial to the good work. When people care, it's everything. You can rehearse and rehearse and rehearse and then you do the fitting and, aha, now I get it. Pat always said it all has to tell the same story. The makeup, the hair, are obviously important. But the clothes are the things that the eye sees, understands and processes first. Great costume designers have been around, good lord,

Interest in horticulture has surged this year. This is a rocky mountain juniper, a popular Long Island perennial. Previous page: a bright, outgoing geranium.

hundreds of years. But with Pat it was so nice to hear them talked about, that people would know their names. People know Patricia Field not just as a cult figure in New York now. The general public got to know the name <u>Manolo Blahnik</u>, too, a Spanish shoe designer, not obscure but known only to a very select few.

P: Manolo is another fabulous storyteller.

S: His was a name that men would shout at me in airports. 'I know you because my wife loves a Manolo!' But they knew. That's kind of sweet.

P: When HBO developed *Girls*, was there ever any sense of melancholy for you that *Sex and the City*'s era was over?

S: I never felt melancholy. There were other shows where women were becoming the focus of stories, the provocation for a story, and I was really proud of HBO for seeking out more female voices, Lena's in particular, who is so gifted and so much her own talent. I was really excited about what she was doing. And that it was a different voice, because her generation was so different. That generation had their own special host of problems and issues, their own language and way of living.

P: How much pressure do you think there was on Lena? She effectively had to be both you and Candace on the *Girls* merry-go-round, the star and the writer the star is based on?

S: It's a lot. It's a huge amount. And I know, because I produced [*SATC*] with Michael. That even was a lot. It was a privileged burden. But she was much younger than me and she was writing it, and it is a machine that is a runaway train. It's just huge. The thing that probably saved her in a lot of ways was that she's at least in touch with herself. She can see where danger exists. She can step in front of it. But she's got better and better at protecting herself and understanding where she just couldn't do something and had to allow someone else to. It's such a big amount for a young woman to be shouldering, you know? I'm enormously impressed by her.

P: She's prodigiously talented.

S: No question. The thing about producing television is that you can't know it until you're in it. If you care, it's all-consuming. And you should care. If you're producing a <u>show on HBO</u>, you've got to care. You can think, I've got it, I've got energy, I'm young. But you won't know until you're in the day-to-day of an actual show running and you're responsible for 200 people, deadlines, budgets, New York, the weather, a sick actor, someone pulling out because they got

6. MANOLO BLAHNIK
—
The designer never trained formally as a shoemaker and indeed studied literature (along with architecture) at the University of Geneva in the 1960s. One of his favourite books is Gustave Flaubert's *Madame Bovary*, for which he designed a limited-edition cover for Penguin Classics in 2006.

7. SHOW ON HBO
—
Parker as Frances Dufresne, a suburban mum whose extramarital affair spells the end of her marriage, in TV show *Divorce* (2016–19).

another job. All the pieces that fit into it are very daunting. She knows it now. But you couldn't before. You can only see that wonderful monster from within it.

P: Another performance that made me think of Carrie Bradshaw, if only because she's the exact inverse of her as both a writer and a woman while at the same time being just as much an essence of West Village New York, is the Melissa McCarthy character in *Can You Ever Forgive Me?*

S: Oh, god, I never saw that. I need to see it.

P: It's a brilliant portrait of a writer on the skids. It wouldn't surprise me at all if she defrauded Three Lives in it. She drinks in Julius, the West Village gay bar.

S: Oh, but I love Julius! Oh my god, I love it. Three Lives is literally across the street from Julius.

P: Can you take me back to yourself on stage with *Annie*? What were your hopes and dreams about acting at 13?

S: This is something that Matthew and I talk about a lot and occasionally share with our children. We just wanted to be actors. How we saw that world was very specific. You were desperate to work in the theatre. Work with good people. Who are the exciting directors? Who is the interesting writer? Who are the actors you just want to stand on the stage with, whether you have two lines or four scenes? Our goal was to work in the theatre. What does that mean? To be able to pay our rent would be fantastic. To have a meal out every now and then? Amazing. To be able to drop the laundry off at the laundromat versus do it yourself? Woah. What characterised and defined success for us was a career in the theatre, as a journeyman. So, when I stood on stage as Annie, I was an actor. I didn't know about fame or wealth or people knowing me beyond the confines of the New York theatre audience. There was no internet. People wrote fan letters. I wrote back to every single one. People were at the stage door. You signed their programme. And then you went home and loaded the dishwasher and swept the floor. I wanted to work and support myself, to leave home at 17 or 18, get my own apartment in New York City and work off-Broadway, on Broadway, off-off Broadway. I didn't care. Point me in the right direction. Tell me what pages to read. I will show up. If I can afford to take a taxi, I will take a taxi. Otherwise I will take a bus or a subway. I could not have been happier. I looked at actors who were ten, twenty years older than me and never thought I'd be their age or have their careers. So that's what I stood on the stage and thought. Could I?

8. MELISSA MCCARTHY CHARACTER
—
This was Lee Israel, in fact a real author who forged and sold a spree of letters by literary figures such as Dorothy Parker and Noël Coward before being arrested by the FBI in 1992. The film is based on, and takes its name from, her confessional memoir.

P: Could you describe your first New York apartment to me?

S: Oh, yes. When I was doing [TV show] *Square Pegs*, I met this man named Timothy Patrick Murphy. He was an actor on the show called *Dallas*. He was a beautiful young man. And he was gay. But he wasn't comfortable or confident being out and publicly gay. This was 1983. We were set up on a date. You can sort of create the proscenium around this relationship. And I loved him. I fell in love with him and very soon was like, hey, wait a minute. We 'broke up', I put in quotes. And we stayed friends. But I still loved him. He was smart, loving and wise, from this wonderful family in Princeton Junction, New Jersey. Irish kid, absolutely beautiful. He got very sick, I would say a week into any public discussion of this 'gay cancer'. He came to me. But before that, he said, 'Listen, I'm living in California but I have an apartment. I'm living on 72nd and Columbus. It's $700 a month,' which was not cheap, but I had just finished *Square Pegs* and I said, 'Oh my gosh, for sure.' I'd just come home from finishing *Footloose*, actually, and was living in my parents' home, but I refused to unpack my suitcases. I'd had a taste of independence. My mom cooked some food and put it in a jar, drove me to New York city and dropped me off. He'd left me the keys at the deli next door. It was a loft over a club called Trax, near a very expensive shoe store called To Boot, opposite a Chemical Bank, a store called Parachute and of course a coffee shop, just down the street from Gray's Papaya, one of my favourite restaurants. I loved it. Everybody rang that bell, my bell, all night long looking for Trax. Timothy came and stayed with me. He said, 'I'm sick.' He was gone within a year and a half of his diagnosis. So, that was my first apartment in New York. It was Timothy's.

P: From the mention of the word 'Dallas' onwards there wasn't a detail of that story that didn't drip with evocative detail.

S: Yeah, that's a story in amber. It's so specific to its time. He was lovely. I was with him to the end. He passed away in Los Angeles at a wonderful hospital in Sherman Oaks where I visited countless more friends, in literally sometimes the exact same room that Timothy was in. A tiny hospital, one of the first places that really took care of the gay community, of people who were dying of AIDS. Timothy was one of the first.

P: I really wasn't expecting this conversation to find its way here.

S: Sorry. Matthew and I have been talking about that time a lot now, because Doctor Fauci has been so much an important part of this [pandemic] conversation for us. Doctor Fauci we all remember from those days of the AIDS crisis. He was such a big, important voice. We all worshipped him then and now he's playing this very crucial role now, if he's allowed to continue.

P: Are you a poetry person at all?

S: No. I read it very occasionally in the *New Yorker*, because that is doable for me. My father was a poet. He graduated from the Iowa Writer's Workshop and he actually started the *American Poetry Review*. Eventually his name was taken off the masthead, maybe in the last five years, because there was some falling out with the original publisher. He toured, like poets did in the late sixties. We would go on tour with him to what I guess now would be college campuses. So, there is poetry in my family, but I don't read it. I think I'm intimidated by it.

P: I'm the same. There are only three poems I love and understand exactly why the words have been chopped up in that formalised way.

S: Sometimes I feel like it's making fun of me, like it's personal. You know who read poetry and loved it was Matthew's mother, who, like my mother was a crazy, crazy reader. We spend time in Ireland and everybody in Ireland can recite anything, any poem. Every child can stand up at a dinner and recite endless poetry from the most important poets of their land. It's humiliating.

P: Another place where storytelling is just in the blood. Irish folk start telling you a story and you are not getting away.

S: And you don't want to! I don't care if they've told me this story a dozen times, which they have. It's never tired or weary. There might be a couple of new details — who cares if they're made up? — the story changes over years, there are added elements that for sure did not exist, but there is nobody better at telling a yarn than any Irish man, or woman or however they might identify.

P: What do you think books have taught you about love?

S: I guess it's the same thing I'd say on the rare occasion when someone asks for advice when they're in agony. When they're much younger than me, I will tell them — and I'm sure this is from books — feel it, don't regret it for one minute. Don't hold back. In five or ten years you will be so grateful for this deep, dark, dreary place you find yourself in. You will long for the day you were staring at your telephone wishing he or she would call. You're better for the heartbreak. Books, before anything, taught me that.

P: One last thing for now. Are you writing a memoir.

S: [explodes laughing] Are you kidding me? No way. Oh, Lordy.

I could never. First of all, I have too much respect for writers to make any attempt to. I don't have the discipline. I'd be afraid, first of all that no one would frankly be that interested and then that they would only be wanting some salacious information, maybe some answers to questions that I have maybe not so coyly chosen not to address. And I can't fulfil just the titillating thing. So, where does that leave me? How do you recall all those details? I never kept a journal. I wouldn't know where to begin.

P: Can I suggest if you ever do, to start with the scene putting your key in the doorway of that first New York apartment? I think you may be surprised at how vividly you can paint the picture of your own life, without the gossip. In the end, that might work to sell a book initially, it might be useful for marketing. But I don't think those details are necessarily what readers want from a famous person's memoir. They just want to step inside their life, to feel their story.

S: Thank you. We're going to continue this, right?

CALLBACK

Two weeks later, prompt, Sarah Jessica Parker calls once more from her New York home. I later learn from a sweet Instagram post that it is the date of her 23rd anniversary with Matthew Broderick. Because of the forthright, lengthy and lovely nature of the first conversation and several WhatsApp communiqués since, there is no longer any delineation to be drawn between the actor and any role she's played.

There had been some suggestion of switching from telephone to a visual platform for round two. But, in the end, the subterfuge of talking on a good, old-fashioned device felt somehow more correct for the times. Of all the oddness of the pandemic, that speaking to someone without seeing their face became so special held an almost otherworldly magic.

Besides, I know exactly what Sarah Jessica Parker's face looks like. You do too. I didn't want to throw her quiet certainty at talking about stories, the epic romance of her love affair with words distractedly off-scent by trying to figure out mine. And who, in all honesty, by 19 May could cope with any more Zoom-time?

P: Since we last spoke, one piece of literature which talks to both your love of literature and of Ireland has become a major phenomenon.
    S: Is it the Sally Rooney?

P: It is. Have you seen *Normal People* on screen?
    S: I haven't yet. But what's really interesting to me about it is that it speaks to her incredible ability to be absolutely random in connecting with readers. There are people I've heard from who relate to the show who don't relate to one another at all. It's not one demographic. It's also very exciting to see a writer who managed to protect work in translation to a different medium, which is so hard. The entertainment industry is littered with exquisite books that were bought, then destroyed, never made it or fell apart. *The Goldfinch* could've been, without exploiting it, in my opinion, three seasons of television, taking apart every detail of that perfect book. So, to see Sally Rooney's book and the writing be so honoured, well, I haven't seen it yet but I'm sure I will. I've heard that people have been happily undone by it. They like the way it hurts.

P: Have you read it?

S: Yes, and *Conversations with Friends*. I literally gobbled them up. I actually had an occasion to meet with her. We were brought together by a mutual friend in publishing before her second book came out. I had read and was completely gobsmacked by it, so I did my best to try to convey to her how impressed I was. She's a wonder.

P: Have you ever been starstruck by meeting a writer?

S: Oh, often. Yes. We have friends that are writers, great writers but I'm over being starstruck by them because they're friends in our lives, you know? But writers of novels I'm meeting more and that's the one where I find myself more at a loss for words, or sincerely starstruck. Sally Rooney, Donna Tartt.

P: Did you meet Donna?

S: I did and I feel I've not tended to it properly, only because I feel like I'm sincerely not able yet to be myself with her. I love her. I think she's amazing, partly because of her mysterious quality, the way she goes away for ten years at a time. Just superficially, she's really beguiling. Her looks, her sartorial efforts. I met Colson Whitehead and managed to completely mangle that. I read *The Nickel Boys* early, maybe six months before it came out and was completely undone by that book. Then a bunch more I've messed up and regretted and wished I could do all over again. I don't know what it is about novelists that makes me swoon.

P: What about a writer from history you'd have loved to have an audience with?

S: I love Evelyn Waugh so much. I love Trollope so much. At the same time, by the way, nothing's more satisfying than being completely absorbed into a heart-breaking Dickens. What's better than that?

P: Do you have a favourite Dickens?

S: I'm trying to think of the one that Matthew and I read aloud to one another, the entire book, in Ireland.

P: Did you read it one chapter each?

S: We took it in turns until we couldn't read anymore. We would go to sleep and start again the next day. It was *Great Expectations*.

P: Is it more or less complicated on first meeting somebody romantically when you have an idea of who they are from fictitious roles first?

S: When I met Matthew, I had seen everything he had done, and I don't know how that had happened. When I was shooting *Footloose*,

9. DONNA TARTT
—

The Goldfinch author is both famously reclusive and a literary fashion icon, favouring menswear-inspired outfits involving pinstripe suits, trench coats and bright ties on those rare occasions she does make a public appearance.

10. FOOTLOOSE
—

Parker as Rusty, best friend of our rebellious heroine Ariel, in musical drama film *Footloose* (1984).

two of his movies came out that summer, if I have my timings correct. I rented a bicycle in Utah, where we were shooting, and rode my bicycle to the movie theatre. I think, strangely, that because I had seen so much of him I didn't have an idea of him. I'd seen him play so many different things. I had seen a bunch of different things, so I couldn't decide who he was. I think the thing in my head was, Oh, he's a New Yorker. And what does *that* mean?

P: What preconceptions do you think he came to you with?

S: I'm not sure. And I have never gotten to the bottom of it. I'm not sure how much he had seen me in.

P: What's the first book you'd save in a house fire?

S: It's hard because I have been thinking about this. The New York Public Library is doing something right now, needing help and reaching out. It's celebrating its 125 years, which is incredible. They've asked me and countless others to select our favourite book, which is just impossible, right? It's like picking a favourite friend. I will say this, there is a book that I have given credit to as being the book that got me into publishing. *A Constellation of Vital Phenomenon* by Anthony Marra. It was 2012, maybe 2013, and I was searching for another book, *The Dinner* by Herman Koch, which hadn't yet been published in America. I was calling bookstores and pretending to be a publicist, a publisher, a press agent. I would be like, 'Hello, this Miriam Grossman, I wonder if you have a copy of Herman Koch's *The Dinner.*' Then the editor of *Cosmopolitan* calls me and invites me to what she says is 'an intimate lunch at Michael's'. She says it's just going to be a few women. So, I take a cab up to midtown to Michael's, don't have a stitch of makeup on and there's paparazzi everywhere. I walk in the door and it's literally a hundred women all in power suits. I'm in a dress I got online. After the lunch is over, we're walking towards the exit and this young woman comes over and says, 'I want to introduce myself, I'm Molly Stern and I'm a publisher at Crown. This is Gillian Flynn, you were photographed with her book, *Gone Girl*.' We started talking and it turns out she is publishing *The Dinner* for Hogarth, this new imprint for Crown. She says to me, 'I'll send it to you.' Oh my god. I get her card, email her to say thank you, I'm so excited and she sends me a stack of books. I can't believe I've got my hands on *The Dinner* by now — it's like contraband — and in this stack of books is *A Constellation of Vital Phenomenon*. Why I picked this book up first is beyond me. But I am so stunned by this book, I can't even tell you. I think it's maybe one of the most important books of our time, by this debut writer. It's a heartrending book about Chechnya. I'm a third, maybe two thirds into it, email Molly, saying I'm reading this book by your author, Mr Marra, I've never read anything like it in my life and I cannot believe how good it is. I said I've no idea what I can do, but if there is any way I can help this book, this very hard subject — how do you market a book about Chechnya by a brand new author? — I want to do anything I can. From that, we become friends and start this book club, just about unpublished books. Anthony comes to speak to us at the first book club. A few days after, Molly asked me: would you start publishing books? She convinced me I could manage it. And my gold standard when looking through manuscripts has always been *A Constellation of Vital Phenomemon*. So, when someone asks me, what is your favourite book? Anthony's book is always there.

P: How did publishing change the way you saw yourself?

S: When I came to the UK to talk about the first book, Fatima's book [*A Place for Us* by Fatima Farheen Mirza], I said to the publicist, Oh my gosh, it is so much easier to be interviewed as a publisher than it is an actor. Because the interviews take on a serious tone immediately. No one's asking me about the internecine battles on the set of *Sex and the City*. They're asking me about a writer and a story. It's so refreshing, but also sort of heart-breaking to see the difference between approaches from the very moment someone sits down. It changed the way I wanted to conduct press for things I cared about. To maybe speak to people who didn't come in ready for a secret argument, for some kind of battle.

P: Has fame been good to you?

S: In a million ways. I'm more grateful than anything. But there are things that are challenging and it's my job to meet the challenge and try to neutralise it in some way that isn't argumentative, antagonistic or confrontational. There are things you come up against as an actor. Listen, in no way is this a competitive cross to bear. I don't think like that. I try to recognise it and how I might handle it better or just accept it, you know?

P: There was an expression that you used in the first conversation we had which has stayed with me for the last two weeks. I can't stop thinking about your description of a good book as 'the most eloquent way of screaming'.

S: Yes.

P: It's perfect. Do you want to elaborate on that or would you rather let those words hang in the ether and find their own temperature?

S: Why don't you let them sit? If you want to talk again, I'm at your beck and call.

PAUL FLYNN is one of the Senior Editors at Love, author of *Good As You* (Ebury Press, 2017) and *Grazia* magazine TV columnist of 15 years standing. His favourite instalment of *Sex and The City* is Season 1, Episode 12, 'Oh Come All Ye Faithful', affectionately known among fans as 'The Catholic Guy Episode'.

The eldest of Parker's three children has the middle name 'Wilkie', after English novelist Wilkie Collins.

32

STAFF PICKS

Parker's favourite bookstore Three Lives & Company is on a corner in the West Village by gay bar Julius and ice cream shop Van Leeuwen. The staff are just brilliant, so what are their latest book tips?

THE REDEMPTION OF GALEN PIKE: AND OTHER STORIES (2014)
Carys Davies

'My all-time favourite short story collection, full stop. I read these stories years ago, and I plan to reread them on a regular basis, but I find myself still turning them over in my mind and reflecting on their brilliance and power.' (Selected by Miriam Chotiner-Gardner)

GO, WENT, GONE (2017)
Jenny Erpenbeck (tr. Susan Bernofsky)

'Erpenbeck's writing is intense, unflinching, and remarkably touching as she examines the refugee crisis from all angles, reminding us of what it means to be human and our obligation to do better.' (Selected by Nora Shychuk)

HEATING & COOLING (2017)
Beth Ann Fennelly

'In fifty-two so-called "micro memoirs" and under 120 pages, Beth Ann Fennelly assembles a laugh-out-loud funny, surprising, and quite moving portrait of her life, featuring her relationships with her husband, children, mother, sister, and friends. She needs so few words to convey her stories and insights with such grace, spark, and humour. I only wished to spend many more pages in Fennelly's company.' (Selected by Miriam Chotiner-Gardner)

A BRIEF HISTORY OF SEVEN KILLINGS (2014)
Marlon James

'It's about the mean streets of Kingston, Jamaica in the 1970s, and the outskirts of Brooklyn a decade later. It's about gangsters, secret agents, prostitutes, journalists, and the fifty-odd bullets that nearly killed Bob Marley at age 31. It's an epic mash-up of reggae and drugs, narrated by such a memorable cast of voices that the lowest-grade political thugs are characters every bit as alive and realised as Marley himself.' (Selected by Ryan Murphy)

STRANGE WEATHER IN TOKYO (2013)
Hiromi Kawakami (tr. Allison Markin Powell)

'A quiet novel about a slow relationship that Kawakami develops so subtly and ten-derly that the meeting of two lonely hearts seems beautifully preordained.' (Selected by Ryan Murphy)

A MEAL IN WINTER (2013)
Hubert Mingarelli (tr. Sam Taylor)

'A breathtakingly powerful little novel about three German sol-diers, who, seeking to avoid horrifying duties back at camp, venture into the Polish countryside on a brutally cold winter day during the Second World War. By late afternoon, this excursion has led them to a defining moment in their lives.' (Selected by Toby Cox)

THE FORGIVEN (2012)
Lawrence Osborne

'The place is Morocco. The setting is a party. A couple from Lon-don have accepted the invitation, but on the way two young men spring from the roadside — one is struck, and the other runs into the hills. It's from here, as the couple arrives at the party with the dead body in the car, that Osborne's stunning novel unfolds and takes us on a dark, psy-chological journey.' (Selected by Joyce McNamara)

SERGIO Y. (2016)
Alexandre Vidal Porto (tr. Alex Ladd)

'The less you know about this novel from the outset, the better. Porto is a leading figure in Brazil's "New Urban" fiction movement, and *Sergio Y.* is proof alone that superb literature is coming out of Brazil.' (Selected by Troy Chatterton)

Three Lives & Company
154 West 10th St
New York City, NY 10014
USA
(+1) 212 741 2069

Open 10am to 8.30pm every day except Sunday, when it's open but only from 12pm to 7pm.

THE HAPPY
READER

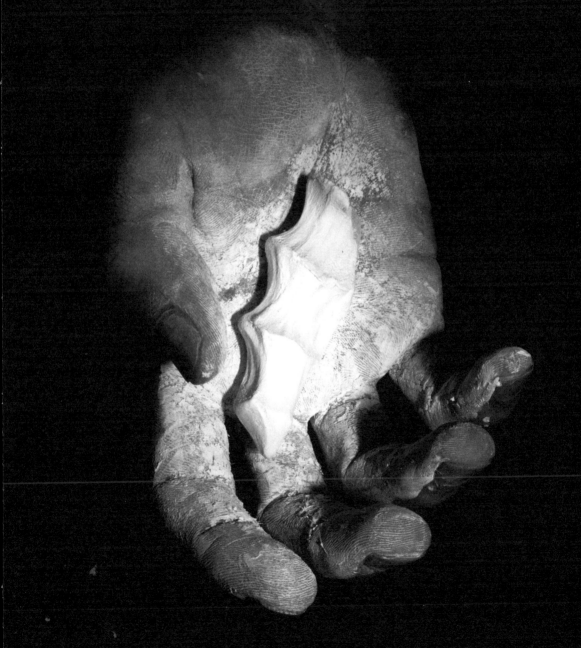

Both a paranormal treasury and a mirror image of their author, the JAPANESE GHOST
STORIES of Lafcadio Hearn are our Book of the Season this abnormal autumn.

VISIONS

What is a ghost story? Photographer LIEKO SHIGA here presents a new series in response to Lafcadio Hearn's *The Story of Mimi-Nashi-Hōïchi*. Shooting in Miyagi prefecture in the northeast of Japan, Shiga takes inspiration from a tale in which a blind singer accidentally performs for the undead — a dangerous mistake. 'It's interesting,' says Shiga, 'that stories telling readers to imagine such truly horrifying things have been passed down from old times.'

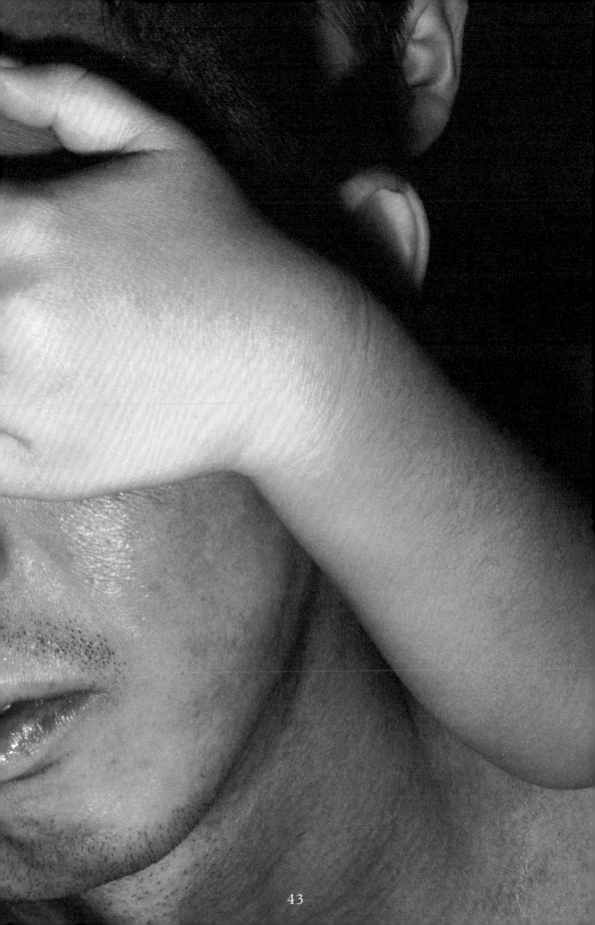

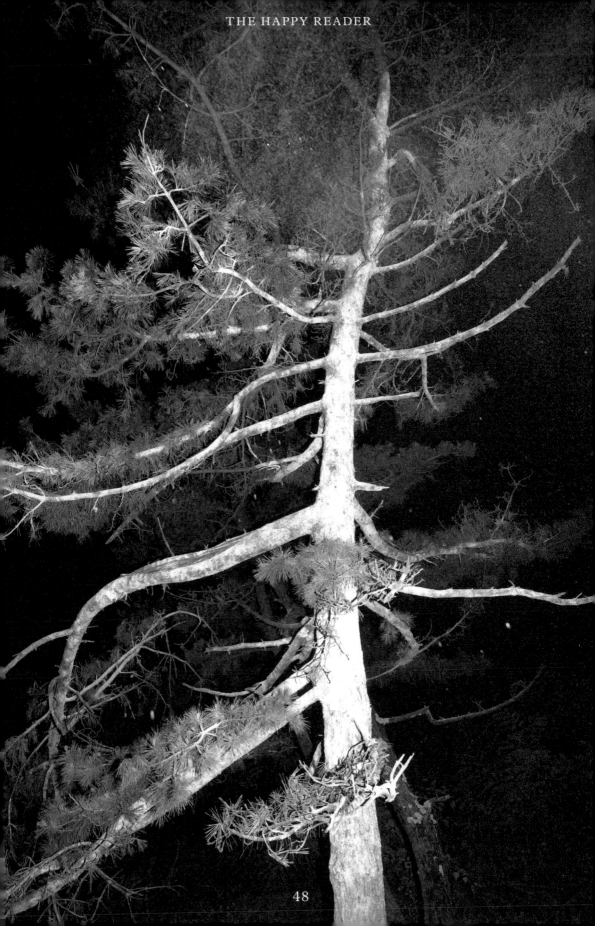

FIVE SCENES IN LAFCADIO HEARN'S CRAZY LIFE

The chilling vignettes collected in *Japanese Ghost Stories* were written towards the end of Lafcadio Hearn's life, a time when he was not only describing Japan to Western readers but becoming part of its culture in his own right. But just exactly how does someone go from being born in a Mediterranean archipelago in 1850 to showing up decades later a proud and indeed traditionally-inclined citizen of Japan? At other times, in different places — the French Quarter of New Orleans for example — Hearn had led many other lives: a crime reporter, a restaurateur, a novelist, a vagrant. In the pages to come a series of →

49

→ contributors assemble a portrait of this whimsically-weird phantom chronicler. It all starts, writes SEB EMINA, one Thursday on an occupied island near Greece. Hearn would never have existed were it not for an unlikely love affair. He'd have been much happier, and we'd have likely never heard of him, if he'd just stayed put on the island that named him.

BORN — Lefkada, also known as Lefkas or Santa Maura, is on the edge of the Ionian Sea. It is only just about an island, being close enough to the Greek mainland to be reached by car: a dramatic causeway links the main town or *chora* with the region of Acarnania. Lefkada is sweltering in summer and not especially cold in winter. Inasmuch as it's possible to count residents in a land of touristic flux, it has a population of 22,652. Attractions include breathtaking beaches, a flamingo-filled lagoon, and several understated hauntings by the author Lafcadio Hearn.

There is a statue, a small museum, an eponymous street — discreet breadcrumbs for those in the know, marking the fact that he began his life here, on 27 June 1850.

Back then Lefkada was part of the United States of the Ionian Islands, a British protectorate of seven territories also including Zakynthos, Corfu and Kythira. 'The only amusements the island affords are fishing and shooting,' said a nineteenth-century travel guide. 'There is no hotel.' Lafcadio's mother was from an important family in Kythira. His father, an army surgeon, arrived as part of a British troop expansion, following an uptick in revolutionary stirrings.

Rosa, 25, and Charles, 30, met and fell in love after the latter approached the former on a street in a Kythiran village. Rosa Kassimati was — Lafcadio would write — 'of little stature, with black hair and black eyes'. She was incredibly pious but also ardently independent, a rare trait on an island where women's lives were far from free. Charles Hearn was a great swordsman, had long sideburns, and liked to write romantic songs. Their story, though filled with the right kind of adversity (as in the external sort, to be overcome), only ever threatened to resolve itself into a happy ending. In the more operatic version, Rosa's brother Demetrius, who found the match dishonourable, knifed Charles repeatedly in an alleyway. When news of the attack reached her, Rosa rushed to the spot where Charles lay bleeding in the dust. She nursed him back to health in a cave.

The couple ran away to Lefkada and had a baby son named George. Soon afterwards Charles received new orders: he would be reposted to the West Indies. Before he left, they were married at a small ceremony carried out by a Greek Orthodox priest. No family were present.

Rosa became pregnant again. The island suffered from outbreaks of disease — 'intermittent fevers' as the travel guide put it — and George became gravely ill. There was nothing anyone could do: he

1. HIS BIRTHPLACE

'I have memory of a place and a magical time in which the Sun and the Moon were larger and brighter than now. Whether it was of this life or of some life before I cannot tell. But I know the sky was very much more blue, and nearer to the world – almost as it seems to become above the masts of a steamer steaming into equatorial summer. The sea was alive, and used to talk – and the Wind made me cry out for joy when it touched me. Once or twice during other years, in divine days lived among the peaks, I have dreamed just for a moment that the same wind was blowing – but it was only a remembrance.

'And all that country and time were softly ruled by One who thought only of ways to make me happy. Sometimes I would refuse to be made happy, and that always caused her pain, although she was divine; and I remember that I tried very hard to be sorry. When day died before his first birthday. Riven by grief and without Charles to support her, Rosa devoted herself to the baby boy she'd given birth to just two months beforebefore, whose name was Patrick Lafcadio. She carried him around the island on a donkey. Sometimes they ambled up to a cliff where the ruins of a temple to Apollo were found among the cypress trees, and from which could be seen the island of Ithaca, home of the world's most famous traveller, Odysseus.

When Lafcadio was two years old, Rosa received a summons. It was time to leave the island for Dublin. Charles was still serving in the empire but the family thought it best if wife and child were absorbed into the Hearns. Which is how Lafcadio came to leave his birthplace and set off on a westward journey, that would, in a sense, never end.

Decades later in Japan he would write 'The Dream of a Summer Day', a travelogue in which is stowed a pair of ancient ghost stories. One, the story of Urashima Tarō, is about the consequences of not being able to decide where home is. The other, an old unnamed legend, is about what happens when a person drinks too deeply from the fountain of youth.

Between them is found an extraordinary authorial interjection about 'a place and a magical time in which the Sun and the Moon were larger and brighter than now' and which was 'softly ruled by One who thought only of ways to make me happy'. This passage, just two paragraphs long, tends to stop readers in their tracks. It appears in every biography. It's as if Lafcadio's entire psyche is contained in it somehow, that his life story is an elaborate crossword clue, the answer to which has been revealed to be simply 'Lefkada'.

> was done, and there fell the great hush of the light before moonrise, she would tell me stories that made me tingle from head to foot with pleasure. I have never heard any other stories half so beautiful. And when the pleasure became too great, she would sing a weird little song which always brought sleep. At last there came a parting day; and she wept, and told me of a charm she had given that I must never, never lose, because it would keep me young, and give me power to return. But I never returned. And the years went; and one day I knew that I had lost the charm, and had become ridiculously old.'
> Lafcadio Hearn, 'The Dream of a Summer Day' (1894)

What happens next? Belfast-based writer JOHN SELF traces Hearn's Irish adolescence, a painful time and the origins of certain entrenching tendencies, from abandonment issues to a fixation with grotesquery and horror.

ABANDONED — 'I ought to love Irish things, and I do,' wrote Lafcadio Hearn to W. B. Yeats in 1901. To which we might reply: well, to a point. His full name was Patrick Lafcadio Hearn, and he was known as Paddy as a young man, until he abandoned it for his middle name, making him unplaceably exotic and definitely not Irish any longer.

The truth is that Hearn felt deeply ambivalent towards Ireland, the only childhood home he knew, yet it was also deeply influential on the work he's celebrated for. He had a comfortable upbringing in affluent south Dublin, in a house so well-appointed that the high beds needed steps for him to reach them. But Hearn's childhood in Ireland was tempest-tossed. He was taken there and then abandoned, first by his mother, then by his father, and his younger brother was taken away from him.

Two-year-old Hearn was an unusual sight in nineteenth-century Dublin, with black shoulder-length hair and gold earrings, in his own words a 'perfect imp', playing practical jokes on his family: a needle protruding from a chair, a bottle of ink balanced on a door.

But his mother Rosa suffered mental ill-health — she once had to be physically restrained from jumping through a window — and returned to her native Greece alone, for ever, when Hearn was four. His father, Charles, left Ireland permanently in 1857, so Hearn was raised by an elderly great-aunt, Sarah Brenane, who referred to him impersonally as 'the Child'.

In his Irish childhood we see the grains of Hearn's future interest in the occult and the supernatural. Holidays were in the seaside village of Tramore, where he was told folk tales by a local fisherman; when he embellished these stories for the benefit of his nurse, he was punished. And his interest in the otherworldly and strange resulted in clashes with his deeply religious great-aunt. Once, forced to go to confession, he admitted (truthfully) to the priest that he wished for the devil to come to him in the form of beautiful women, and that he should yield to their temptations. This resulted in the priest leaping to his feet and screaming threats, which Hearn considered not discouraging but quite the opposite, for the priest's reaction was so extreme that Hearn thought there must be some prospect of his desires coming true.

Despite his interest in devilish things, Hearn was terrified of the dark, and his great-aunt viewed this as a disorder to be corrected, using the guerrilla therapy of — what else? — locking the boy in a pitch-black bedroom. Hearn wrote with vivid horror about this experience in an essay entitled 'Nightmare-Touch'. When the light was switched off and door locked, 'the agony of fear would come upon me,' and 'something in the black air would seem to gather and grow — (I thought that I could hear it grow).' Worse, he could hear the happy voices in the room next door, a world away, while his imagination tormented him with dark-robed figures crossing the walls and ceiling, while he was literally paralysed with terror. Eventually, when he could bear it no longer, he screamed out for help.

Screaming brought punishment (candle, strap), but it also brought back the light, which was all Hearn wanted. His imagination made the shapes he sensed so alive that he *could not* accept adult explanations that they were not real. It took maturity, and distance, for Hearn to be able to value what he called 'the pleasure of fear' and to harness his own frightening imaginative power to create something lurid and true, but, when he did — in the peculiar vivid directness of his Japanese ghost stories — we are all the beneficiaries.

In Dublin he would spend time poring over illustrated books on Greek mythology in the family library ('I loved them! I adored them!'). To them he attributed his understanding of beauty and the sublime: they were simultaneously thrilling and fear-inducing. But to his pious great-aunt these ancient gods were idolatrous, friends of the devil. This just made them more appealing to Hearn, who was so thoroughly fed up with his family's restrictive, judgemental God that he felt 'a natural sympathy with his enemies' — as the family priest had already discovered.

Worse still from his great-aunt's point of view, the Greek gods in the books were often naked. When it was discovered that young Hearn had been looking at these books they were taken away, and returned with the offending body parts cut away (one beautiful figure had her breasts removed with a pen knife) or — in a stroke of unintentional comic brilliance — covered up by underwear drawn on with a quill pen, including 'large baggy bathing drawers'. This didn't have the slightest

2. HIS NIGHTMARES

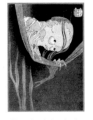

'The dark had always been peopled for me with shapes of terror. So far back as memory extended, I had suffered from ugly dreams; and when aroused from them I could always see the forms dreamed of, lurking in the shadows of the room. They would soon fade out; but for several moments they would appear like tangible realities. And they were always the same figures...

discouraging effect on Hearn, who developed his drawing skills by trying to trace the lines of the limbs beneath the scribbled-on clothing.

But now, perhaps, we can begin to understand Patrick's ambivalence towards his Irish childhood. And little wonder that he longed for his mother, of whom he had little memory but — therefore — strong devotion. He saw Rosa as the source of all his best qualities, and continued to see her in visions, which led to a 'rash desire to wander over the world in search of something like her'.

He longed for the exoticism represented by his mother with her Greek heritage; Ireland, as his childhood home, could never fulfil that psychic need. He would wander over the world, changing his name — and so his identity — several times.

And what remains of Patrick Lafcadio Hearn in Ireland? For a time, there was nothing. But in recent years a plaque was erected at 73 Upper Leeson Street in Dublin, that well-appointed house where he lived with his great-aunt. Then, in 2015, the Lafcadio Hearn Japanese Gardens were opened in the village of Tramore, on Ireland's south-east coast, where Hearn spent so many childhood summers.

A few minutes from the Gardens lies Tramore Strand, the beautiful three-mile stretch of beach for which the village is famous, and where Charles Hearn took seven-year-old Patrick for a walk 'on a very hot day' in July 1857. He never saw his father again.

Sometimes, without any preface of dreams, I used to see them at twilight-time,—following me about from room to room, or reaching long dim hands after me, from storey to storey, up through the interspaces of the deep stairways.'
Lafcadio Hearn, 'Nightmare-Touch', 1900

Hearn attended Catholic schools in Normandy and Durham, which he did not love, and then was sent to live in the East End of London. Some rewarding times in the library aside, that didn't go well for him either. In the end his family abandoned him again, or rather forced him to abandon them, courtesy of a one-way trip to the USA, where he eventually washed up in Cincinnati. At which point, as TRAVIS ELBOROUGH here details, he found his calling as a fearless reporter with a gift for the strange.

HIRED — At 4 o'clock on 25 May 1876, Lafcadio Hearn, then working as a newspaper man in Cincinnati, Ohio, embarked on perhaps his most daring journalistic assignment: the ascent of that city's tallest building, the cathedral of St Peter-in-Chains. Hearn was five foot three, slight and feline, with olive skin and a mop of jet black hair falling over a square forehead, and sporting a droopy Zapata-style moustache. Known to his friend and mentor the English printer Henry Watkins as the Raven, because of his rather sinister appearance and a penchant for the macabre, no one would ever mistake him for an urban climber.

There was also the small matter of Hearn having been blind in one eye since childhood and being so shortsighted in the other that he required a magnifying glass to read his own copy. Hearn credited his myopia with giving him an eye for the 'enormous and lurid', his 'insect vision' a boon helping him to spot what other writers could only turn a merely metaphorical blind eye to. But even Hearn could not have missed St Peter-in-Chains when he'd first come to Cincinnati six years earlier, with its spire in pure white limestone towering more than two hundred feet above him.

After a spell in New York, Hearn had arrived in Cincinnati in 1870, knowing no one but with the understanding that he would receive some family money from a distant relation, an Irishman name Cullinane. If Hearn nursed any expectations of a warm welcome, these were quickly disabused. Cullinane proved entirely indifferent to the new émigré and, after doling out the promised five dollars, bluntly told him to fend for himself. What followed were some exceedingly low times, with Hearn forced to sleep on the city's streets, forage for food, bunk in haylofts and hide in abandoned grocery-store boxes to avoid being arrested for vagrancy. Fortunately, he met Watkins, who took him under his wing, gave him a roof over his head and work in his printshop, and set him on his way as a journalist.

*** Skull and Crossbones ***

Hearn's passage to the summit of the spire of St Peter-in-Chains was achieved on the shoulders of a publicity-hungry steeplejack called Joseph Rodriguez Weston, who'd challenged the city's journalists to join him on the climb. As Hearn subsequently reported, Weston was a good Catholic boy, preferring not to climb on Fridays, though he was also a realist who wore braces with skull-and-crossbones buckles to remind him of his eventual, quite probably inevitable, fate in this, his chosen profession. Only Hearn was fearless, or foolhardy, enough to accept the challenge.

The city that Hearn was able to survey from the eyrie of the cathedral spire, which, he wrote, was laid out before him 'like an elaborate map', was at that time America's largest inland city. A riverine settlement of smoking factories whose lifeblood was the Ohio, that great body of water bustling with steamboats, Cincinnati was a midwestern metropolis yet to be surpassed by such regional whippersnappers as Chicago or St Louis. It was dubbed the Queen City by its boosters, who pointed to its two opera houses, its theatres, its newspapers and its elegant monuments as evidence of its superior character.

But then Hearn, as Cincinnati's most intrepid newshound, knew better than anyone that, beyond the neat squares and broad avenues of its more genteel quarters, this was a city of largely unfettered, often insanitary, sudden growth: a place teeming with 216,000 souls and intermittently afflicted by lethal outbreaks of cholera.

Cincinnati, almost as ethnically mixed as Hearn himself, had a working adult population over half of which was foreign born. A fifth of its inhabitants were German, largely occupying a district north and east of the Miami Canal known as Over the Rhine. Here they toiled, often in unsavoury conditions, slaughtering pigs and packing pork, manufacturing soap or candles and brewing beer.

3. HIS HEADLINES

– 'A Nasty Nest: A Nameless Alley and Its Nameless Crimes' (*Cincinnati Enquirer*, July '73)
– 'Almost a Riot: A Saturday Night Stirring Up of the Sixth Street Slums' (*Cincinnati Enquirer*, August '73)
– 'The Mysterious Man: The Sort of Stuff Some Spiritualists Can Stomach' (*Cincinnati Enquirer*, February '74)
– 'Barbarous Barbers: A Chat with a Tonsorial Professor: How the Chin-Raspers of Cincinnati are Paid' (*Cincinnati Enquirer* March '74)

It was the murder in this district in 1874 of Herman Shilling, a young German working in Frieberg's tannery on Lexington Street and Gamble Alley, that gave Hearn his first big break as a reporter. His dispatches on the so-called 'Tanyard Murder' for the *Cincinnati Enquirer* gripped the city. Sparing few details of the killing and its perpetrators' attempts to incinerate the victim's body, Hearn related the dreadful events with a suspenseful pacing and a Gothic turn of phrase that were the equal of those in tales by his beloved Edgar Allan Poe.

*** O'Hearn ***

Most of the cops whose beats Hearn tailed as the *Enquirer*'s dogged 'night station' man were Irish. (Recognising him as one of their own they nicknamed him O'Hearn.) The Irish community was the other most sizeable group in Cincinnati, though there were also pockets of French, English, Italians, Greeks and Chinese, and a small Jewish community as well.

Cincinnati was also home to thousands of African-Americans, almost all of whom were ex-slaves, most living in the area below Fourth Street and jammed into the shanties of Bucktown, near the sixth and seventh streets of Broadway, or further down still in the flood-prone riverside shacks and waterfront warehouse cellars of the Bottoms, or Levee. Nevertheless, they were probably glad enough to be free of the former bondage in Kentucky just across the Ohio River. This watery borderline, which once separated the slave-owning south from the northern 'free' city, making Cincinnati the first stop on the Underground Railroad (the secret network that enabled slaves to escape to the north), had been spanned since the American Civil War by John A. Roebling's majestic Covington—Cincinnati bridge. On its opening in 1866, it was the longest suspension bridge in the world and a statement, like the construction three years later of the Southern Railway, running from Cincinnati to Chattanooga, of the city fathers' civic and commercial intent. But both constructions also underlined Cincinnati's economic dependency on the one-time southern slave states and the city's always somewhat conflicted moral compass in matters of trade and race.

*** First Marriage ***

Hearn's refusal to accept the prevailing racial prejudices of polite Cincinnati society would lead to his dismissal from the *Enquirer* on the grounds of 'deplorable moral habits'. His sin was to marry Alethea 'Mattie' Foley, a freed slave of mixed race. Hearn had met Foley, who was born on a plantation near Maysville, Kentucky, when she was working as a cook in the cheap boarding house where he was living. Their relationship blossomed over conversations in the kitchen; the journalist preferred to eat his meals there, away from the main dining room and the exhausting rounds of false niceties with other residents.

Foley introduced Hearn to the riverfront black dance houses of the Levee, frequented by roustabouts, whose stories, poems and songs he'd collect and write about. She later appeared, anonymously, in one of Hearn's pieces, 'Some Strange Experience', relating her encounters with ghosts.

- 'Cremation: The Views of a Cincinnati Undertaker: A Man Who Can Reduce You to Ashes for $5' (*Cincinnati Enquirer*, April '74)
- 'Dance of Death: An Enquirer Reporter in a Dissecting Room' (*Cincinnati Enquirer*, May '74)
- 'Some Strange Experience: The Reminiscences of a Ghost-Seer, Being the Result of a Chat on the Kitchen-Stairs' (*Cincinnati Commercial*, September '75)
- 'Levee Life' (*Cincinnati Commercial*, March '76)
- 'Horror on Court Street: Bloody Work of a Liquor-Crazed Lover' (*Cincinnati Commercial*, August '76)

For the couple to marry, illegal under state miscegenation laws, Hearn had to falsely claim Foley was white. After struggling to find anyone willing to perform the ceremony, the couple were eventually married by a black Episcopalian Minster in the home of one of Foley's friends. The union was not a success, and the couple separated after a few months. Hearn's sacking at the *Enquirer* occurred nearly a year after the marriage was over. His initial response was to try to throw himself into the Miami Canal, but within a month he was hired by the *Enquirer*'s daily rival, the *Cincinnati Commercial*, where he wrote some of his finest pieces about the city, not least his sketches of Levee life and 'Steeple Climbers'. But the incident and the racism underpinning it increased his growing disillusionment with the city, whose chilly winters, while once providing him with material for an item on the subject of frost, he found as hard to stomach as the attitudes of a large section of its white inhabitants.

*** Payback ***

Before he left, Hearn was to undertake a crowning act of revenge. For while he was up at the top of St Peter-in-Chains, he took the opportunity to piss on the city from this great height, quite literally. This minor fact of having 'piddled on the universe', as he delicately put it to a friend, was omitted from his published piece.

'It is time to get out of Cincinnati,' wrote Hearn, 'when they start calling it the Paris of America.' With his Ohio self now feeling like an ill fit, the recent divorcé and rising man of letters relocated yet again. Though perhaps it didn't feel like that seeing as he had always lived a little in the realm of ghosts. That tendency is here evoked by BESS LOVEJOY in a new fiction informed by substantive research into Hearn's New Orleans days, and the longstanding fascination of the author herself with that semi-mythical city on the Lower Mississippi.

POSSESSED — In the final months of 1880, Lafcadio Hearn was living in a ruined house in the French Quarter of New Orleans. Jagged cracks pierced the façade; inside, the walls were green with age and always clammy. A small menagerie of cats, chickens, rabbits and dogs prowled the overgrown yard, which buzzed with insects all summer. On the bottom floor lived a fortune-teller, who kept her apartment dark, except for two taper candles burning next to two human skulls.

Hearn was doing OK then, for his American years. At least, he wasn't starving. He'd arrived in New Orleans two years earlier and immediately fallen in love. The city was like a hundred European cities and yet like no other city on Earth: the architecture reminded him of London and Marseilles, while the warm, jasmine-scented air and mélange of accents evoked a tropical seaport. The fact that the place was half in ruins appealed to him, too. The city 'was like young death, — a dead bride crowned with orange flowers,' he wrote to Henry Watkin, his friend and former employer back in Cincinnati, in letters decorated with drawings of a raven, his symbol for himself.

But these intoxicating initial impressions gave way to grinding poverty when his assignments to write about New Orleans for the Cincinnati *Commercial* did not go as planned. Soon, Hearn was wandering the streets, eating only every other day, his face hollowing out. He fell ill with dengue, which clawed at his muscles with iron fingers. By some miracle, the Creole servants at a boarding house nursed him back to health with steaming reddish teas. Determined to chronicle the fast-fading local lore, he offered his nurse money in exchange for her recipe, but she swatted him away. The medicine was *bien dangereuse*, she said, and besides, he wouldn't know where to find the right plants.

The *City Item* hired him when he was on the brink of starvation. By the time he was living above the fortune-teller he was eating well again. Figs for breakfast, with cakes of pressed cream cheese, at a restaurant. Afterwards he went to work at the newspaper, summarizing the news from the telegraphs, writing editorials based on the New York dailies, crafting book reviews, and carving cartoons on the back of old typeset blocks. His work helped the *Item*'s circulation soar, and earned the notice of the city's elite. Yet it did not quite fill the golden afternoons, which he used to haunt second-hand bookshops.

Soon after moving into the house, Hearn grew restless. He began taking long walks, through the narrow lanes of the French Quarter and upriver to the Garden District. He'd go for hours, the air becoming only more fragrant, the trees heavier with fruit, before coming home at 3 or 4 a.m. Perhaps it was after one of these moonlight walks that he first met the fortune-teller. Perhaps not; his notes do not record this part.

Hearn was surprised to discover that the fortune-teller— she said her name was Mamzelle — had a pleasing face with large, hazel eyes. Beneath them, however, lay maroon creases that betrayed a lack of sleep. It turned out they were both insomniacs that autumn, and sometimes, when he came home late at night, she invited him in for a drink. Hearn was collecting Creole lore wherever he could, and soon began bringing small bottles of absinthe, or other herbal spirits, to thank her for the stories she shared.

It was October when they got to talking about voudou. Hearn told her about the St John's Eve ceremonies he'd witnessed on a barge on Lake Pontchartrain, how he'd breathed the heavy scent of incense and flowers piled high on the altars and watched as a graceful woman in a purple dress sprinkled rum over the ecstatic dancers. How when the dancers got too hot, they dived off the barge and into the lake fully clothed, emerging reborn and laughing.

He expected her to be at least mildly impressed by his reminiscences. It had not been easy to find his way on to the barge. But she only smiled sadly.

4. HIS LOOK

'About five feet three inches in height, with unusually broad and powerful shoulders for such a stature, there was an almost feminine grace and lightness in his step and movements. His feet were small and well shaped, but he wore invariably the most clumsy and neglected shoes, and his whole dress was peculiar. His favourite coat, both winter and summer, was a heavy double-breasted "reefer," while the size of his wide-brimmed, soft-crowned hat was a standing joke among his friends. The rest of his garments were apparently purchased for the sake of durability rather than beauty, with the exception of his linen, which, even in days of the direst poverty, was always fresh and good... His hands were very delicate and supple, with quick timid movements that were yet full of charm, and his voice was musical and very soft. He spoke always in short sentences, and the manner of his speech was very modest and deferential. His head was quite remarkably beautiful; the profile both bold and delicate, with admirable modelling of the nose, lips and chin.' Elizabeth Bisland, *The Life and Letters of Lafcadio Hearn* (1906)

5. HIS OMELETTE

'Beat the whites and yolks of six eggs separately, put in a tablespoonful of butter, a spoonful of chopped green onion and one of fine-cut parsley, and mix with the eggs; then put it into a thick-bottomed pan, in which you have placed a half cup of butter. Roll it up as it cooks, and tilt the pan on one side, that the omelette may cook on the other side; roll up again as it cooks. Do not let it get hard and brown, but keep it soft. Keep on rolling as well as you can; a little practice will make you perfect. When the eggs cook, butter, pepper and salt them, and turn on a dish.'
Lafcadio Hearn, *La Cuisine Creole* (1885)

'You are too late for real voudou, I am afraid,' she said. 'These are ceremonies for journalists and curiosity-seekers.' The real worship, she explained, was now almost dead.

'That woman in purple, did you know who she was?' Mamzelle asked.

'They told me that was the voudou queen, Marie Laveau,' Hearn replied. 'And that when it was over, she walked on the water all the way to her cottage on St Anne Street.'

Mamzelle chuckled. 'She can do that, but she probably didn't. And after all, that is not the *real* Marie Laveau — it is her daughter, although she is almost as beautiful as her mother used to be.'

The fortune-teller explained that when she was little, she had played with the young Marie Philomène, Marie Laveau's daughter, during Friday-night ceremonies at the Laveau cottage. The girls would play with ragdolls in a side room, but sneak peeks at the spirit feast in the front of the house, dreaming of being able to eat the cake, the beans and rice.

Hearn's good eye grew wide. He explained that, while he did not wish to trespass on Mamzelle's generosity, he wanted to learn everything he could about voudou, its charms and weird songs. There was one chant in particular that he was trying to decipher — he'd heard his nurse singing it while he convalesced, and its patois reminded him of a family from the Antilles he had once known.

'*Héron mandé, Héron mandé, Ti-gui li pa-pa, Héron mandé, Ti-gui li pa-pa ...*'

He sang it for her. She laughed, and shook her head; she did not know what it meant. Yet in the nights that followed, she told him more about voudou, the little she remembered. Of the deities: Papa Limba or La Bas, Daniel Blanc or Blanc Dani, Yon Sue, and Onzancaire. Of the rattlesnake Marie Laveau kept in an alabaster box, the snake that some say had once spoken and convinced Marie to become a priestess.

Eventually Mamzelle also described the basics of several charms. How to scatter dirt before an entrance or leaves before a house, to chalk figures on a wall, to invoke evil, although the magic was not very strong, and could be counteracted with the right kind of chicken. More threatening was the pillow work: charms slipped beneath pillowcases to cause wasting, spells to make the pillow feathers clump into strange creatures that could harm or kill.

One night, after several glasses of absinthe, Mamzelle revealed that the real Marie was in fact still alive. 'She is a very old woman, and she doesn't speak much, but you can learn a lot just by looking at her eyes,' she explained. 'Perhaps she will know about your song, *Héron mandé, Héron mandé ...*'

They went to St Anne Street a week later, carrying bright flowers and small cakes. At the Laveau cottage, children and animals scampered over the worn cypress floor. In one corner, in an ancient rocking chair, sat Marie Laveau. Her yellowed skin sagged, but her eyes still shone.

Mamzelle elbowed Hearn forward and stood next to him as he bent to present the bouquet and cakes. Marie nodded and smiled at them and then glanced up at a younger relative, who took the gifts away. Hearn recognised her as Marie Philomène, the graceful woman in the purple dress from the boat.

Mamzelle pulled up two straw chairs and began speaking to the older Marie in a patois Hearn couldn't understand. The women laughed, and Hearn sensed that he was being appraised somehow. He was feeling slightly shut out when the talk turned to English, and Marie sat forward.

'Young man,' she said in a low, quiet voice, 'I hear you have a question to ask me.'

'Yes, madame,' he said, willing his nervousness to leave him. 'There is a song I should like to know the meaning of.' And Hearn began to sing: 'Héron mandé, Héron mandé, Ti-gui li pa-pa ...'

Marie burst into laughter, the mirth of a much younger woman quaking her small frame.

'That is a love song to my snake,' she said. 'I'm sorry, but my snake and I are the only ones who know what it means.' She glanced at Mamzelle, and the women tittered, and then Mamzelle's eyes flitted to Hearn's by way of silent, but insincere, apology.

Not ready to give up, Hearn buzzed with questions as a child entered the room balancing a silver plate holding cups of coffee. But he could see that Marie was fading, her eyes falling closed and her breath deepening as she sipped and then set down her drink. All at once, she was snoring.

In her closed eyelids, Hearn saw his dreams of the dying South. Not just arcane, candle-lit ceremonies never to be repeated, but the decaying buildings of the French Quarter, the plantations crumbling into the swamps, the seafood-and-cream-laden dishes that took three days to prepare, the honey-coloured women with their bright skirts and kerchiefs selling sweets by the side of the road. All of it swept away by the vast and unceasing machinery of the North, the tides of progress and prosperity that would trample this perfumed land like a black boot trampling a swamp iris.

'Mama is tired,' Marie Philomène said. Mamzelle nodded and glanced at Hearn, and the pair stood to leave. Hearn bowed to Marie Laveau, and thought he saw her stir for just a moment. Even in her sleep, she seemed to be smiling knowingly, the New Orleans secrets of a hundred years kept warm and safe in her still-beating heart.

When she died the following June, Hearn wrote her obituary for the *City Item*. He would leave New Orleans six years later with many of the city's mysteries undeciphered, yet forever changed by his encounters with the place — and with Maire Laveau.

As demand for Hearn's reporting grew, and his status as a literary giant coalesced, commissions arrived from magazines such as *Harper's* taking him further afield. First off, the West Indies, in which he spent two years as a correspondent. Then: Japan, where he gained a teaching position in the city of Matsue, remarried and became, incredibly unusually for the time, a Japanese citizen. Which is when →

→ the *Japanese Ghost Stories* happened. But let's be honest, reading some of his exoticisations from our vantage point of 2020 is not always an easy or comfortable experience. New York- and Tokyo-based writer MOEKO FUJII surveys the perplexing charm of Hearn's final rebirth.

6. HIS EPIPHANY

'Now I believe in ghosts. Because I saw them? Not at all. I believe in ghosts, though I disbelieve in souls. I believe in ghosts because there are no ghosts now in the modern world. And the difference between a world full of ghosts and another kind of world, shows us what ghosts mean and gods ... What made the aspirational in life? Ghosts. Some were called Gods, some Demons, some Angels; — they changed the world for man; they gave him courage and purpose and the awe of Nature that slowly changed into love; — they filled all things with a sense and motion of invisible life — they made both terror and beauty. There are no ghosts, no angels and demons and gods: all are dead. The world of electricity, steam, mathematics, is blank and cold and void.'
Lafcadio Hearn, a letter to Basil Hall Chamberlain (1893)

RESURRECTED — My first acquaintance with Lafcadio Hearn was, I believe, with his ghost. I went to middle school in central Tokyo, which meant that October was old-Japan season, when we brushed off our drab urban glitter and embarked on class trips to rural prefectures, poking around huge castles and shrines. At night we would wait for the teacher to check in on us — eight black-haired girls breathing softly on buckwheat pillows — and for the screen to close. After a second or two, we would heave ourselves up by our elbows and snap on a cellphone light. We'd drag our futons around our heads, and a girl would start telling a ghost story.

There was, usually, one of these girls in every grade. You knew you weren't going to get much sleep in Yoko's room, for Yoko — aged thirteen — was an early master in the art of freaking people out. She made you look at darkness differently — she made it have cold fingers, a tepid, waiting breath — and she could make a wooden creak or an insect on a glass pane seem to prefigure one's doom. One quiet night, Yoko told the story of the ghost of Lafcadio Hearn. Do you know the story of a foreigner with only one eye, who had died, she asked us, long ago, before his time, on Japanese soil? He only appeared in old inns like these, when someone was telling a ghost story. Yes, a ghost that liked to listen to Japanese ghost stories — here she paused for our scared laughter, asking, should she continue with ours? — and you knew he was approaching when you heard a folk song being sung by a man with a foreign accent. Like this. And you had to open your eyes when you heard him, because if you didn't — if you didn't meet his one, green, glinting eye, to let him know you were watching him — he would stick his long fingers into your eye-socket the moment you fell asleep and fish out an eye. That night, just as we all started to nod off, Yoko sang a folk song softly, in a foreigner's Japanese. As her voice faded away, I dredged my covers to my chin and scoured the darkness, scanning for that hard, green glint.

I didn't know then that Yoko had done her homework — we all knew his name, but not the specifics of his person — that the details that she chose to include in her story of Hearn the apparition corresponded with Hearn the man, one of the first interpreters of Japan at the turn of the twentieth century, the essayist, lecturer, journalist, folklorist and writer of Japanese ghost stories who, for decades, held most of the Western world in thrall with tales from Meiji-era Japan. A good ghost story — creating or adapting one, sounding its specific beats — needs a teller who has done their homework. I don't quite know or frankly care what Lafcadio Hearn would've thought about us girls: he had hard and fast generalisations about Japanese women, and even harsher ideas about loud, urban youth. But a part of me thinks he would've liked Yoko — as a meticulous storyteller himself — and her artfulness in turning him into a ghost lured by tales of ghosts.

 When Lafcadio Hearn arrived in Yokohama on 12 April 1890, as a foreign correspondent for *Harper's Magazine*, he found that he'd come to a land of ghosts and witchery. As I read through his early journalism, I write a list on a legal pad of all the stuff he finds 'ghostly': Mount Fuji, flutes, the misty haze of early mornings, lotus blossoms, a cricket, the length of women's hair, the sea, mites, bridges, the sound of wooden clogs and insects, the colour blue. Part of the reason why I did this was to distract myself from making angrier kinds of catalogues in my head. There's a rhapsodic essentialism in Hearn's reports from Japan — 'an Elf-land having a special sun' / 'Oriental heaven' — that never ceases to remind us that we have Hearn, and others following Hearn, to thank for modern-day white boys with samurai swords on their walls. The more I read the more I find: his breathless devotion to an 'old', 'ancient' Japan didn't let up till the day that he died, twenty-four years after his arrival. 'I should like, when my time comes,' he wrote in a late essay in *Kwaidan*, 'to be laid away in some Buddhist graveyard of the ancient kind, — so that my ghostly company should be ancient, caring nothing for the fashions and the changes and the disintegrations of the Meiji.' The aftereffects of the Meiji Revolution, for Hearn, meant too much modernity. The appropriate reaction to this sentence — as has been the reaction of decades of Japanese and European academics — is, 'Wow, yuck'.

But I resist reducing the entirety of his work on Japan to that stale indictment. Perhaps it's because he tackled so many forms — essays, short stories, folklore adaptations, journalistic articles — or perhaps because *there's so much of it*, by a man who spoke Japanese like a five-year-old, couldn't read a newspaper, and loved to stamp around the house singing Japanese folk and military songs with his children. Perhaps it's because I like his discerning crotchetiness, his reliable hate-reads of everything that wasn't 'old Japan', such as the entirety of Tokyo, which he moved to in 1896 and was immediately 'the most horrible place in Japan ... there is no Japan in it' ... only 'dirty shoes, — absurd fashion, — wickedly expensive living — airs, vanities, — gossip'. It drove him inside to a monastic life by his desk, shunning society: Nina Kennard, in a 400-page biography, would comment drily in 1911, 'It is impossible in the space at my command to examine Hearn's work at Tokyo in detail; it consists of nine books.' We are so used to white men who aestheticize Japan from afar, so benumbed to the *Madame Butterfly* narrative — the man who flits to Japan, pens some impressionistic thoughts, finds a lover, then leaves her to go 'back' — but what do we do with the work of white men who *stay*? What do we do with this one-eyed foreigner, who became a Japanese citizen named Yakumo Koizumi?

Perhaps we see him through the words of a woman who did more than love him. In 1890, he arrived in Matsue, a small city in northwest Japan, where his great-grandson, Bon Koizumi, now runs the Lafcadio Hearn Memorial Museum. After a year there, his health fell apart as he tried to live on soy and beans as a bachelor. A professor-friend intervened, arranging a marriage for him with a twenty-year-old Japanese woman, Setsuko Koizumi. No English-language biography of Hearn or essay on him fails to mention, breathlessly, that she was a 'capable daughter of a fallen samurai family' and to leave it at that, a fact I find the least interesting thing about her. To start with, she was his greatest profiler, a woman who, like Sei Shonagon, could tell the story of a life with a list of sensibilities: 'I name some things that Hearn liked extremely: the west, sunsets, summer, swimming, banana trees, Japanese cedar, lonely cemeteries, insects, ghostly tales, Urashima, and songs. He was fond of beefsteak and plum-pudding, and enjoyed smoking. He disliked liars, abuse of the weak, Prince Albert coats, white shirts, the City of New York, and many other things.'

But what Hearn wrote about Japanese folklore — one of his major legacies, what he would become known for — would certainly not exist had it not been for Setsu. 'On quiet nights,' she wrote in her memoir, 'after lowering the wick of the lamp, I would begin to tell ghost stories.' She saw this as work, *their* work — 'while we were working on this story of 'Miminashi-Yoshi-ichi' — one that was part play, partly a rapture of enduring, cross-cultural love, but also a creative and intellectual endeavour. Hearn loved these ghost stories, she writes, couldn't get enough of them, so she would run from one secondhand bookstore to another, looking for books of old tales to memorize and tell to him. Hearn wouldn't like it when Setsu read from books: he preferred her own words and phrases, her own thoughts. 'Therefore I had to assimilate the story before telling it. That made me dream.' Let's linger for a moment on what skill it takes to 'assimilate' a story, to then tell it to someone who — because of his insistence you learn no English — you must communicate with, and frighten, in a simple Japanese. And as she told him her stories, he would stop her — how was a particular line said? What kind of night was it? How did the wooden clogs sound? He would leap up and demonstrate, asking her what she thought it might've sounded like. And she would show him, and he would take notes. 'Had any one seen us from the outside,' Setsu wrote, 'we must have appeared like two mad people.'

7. HIS SON

'Father was not the kind to overlook natural beauty. Even with his defective eye many things that other people overlooked he would take in — which everyone thought was very strange. Sun, moon, stars, birds, animals, fish, insects, grass, trees, stones, earth — to all these he gave astonishing attention and much interest, and he specially liked to look in the direction where Paradise is supposed to be and admire the beauty of the setting sun. He would sometimes rush out into the garden and call the whole family to come and watch it. I, who was absorbed in play, would be suddenly called away loudly to come and view the evening glow or watch the procession of

I look at Hearn through — is she, too, a ghost? — Setsu, and I revisit my long list of his 'ghostly' Japanese things. I think about his lecture on ghostliness, given to his Japanese students at Tokyo Imperial University, who were devoted to him — we have access to these unrecorded lectures, because many of his students wrote them down, word-for-word — about how he believed that the apprehension of ghostliness was universal, that, no matter what religion, race or creed, we are 'all ghosts of ourselves — and utterly incomprehensible'. All great art, he claimed, had something ghostly in it: it touches us, and we 'feel a thrill in the heart and mind much like the thrill which in all times men felt when they thought they saw a ghost or a god'. But you can't learn to tell the ghostly from reading books, he said. You had to find that feeling in your dreams.

Hearn woke up from a gossamer dream of Japan: 'I can't stand them,' he wrote to Basil Chamberlain as early as 1894, talking of 'Japanese in frock-coats and loud neckties' — 'I must get out of the country for a time.' How fitting it is that Hearn loved the tale of Urashima, a Rip Van Winkle story of a fisherman who travels on a turtle to a timeless dream-palace at the bottom of the sea, only to wake up in reality

ants, or watch the toad swallow mosquitoes. I considered it a nuisance. And what a sin on my part, for at such times my father would show and explain these phenomena, and end by apologising, saying "Sorry to disturb your play, pardon, pardon," and planting a kiss on my cheek, would let me go free.'
Kazuo Koizumi, *Father and I: Memories of Lafcadio Hearn* (1935)

to find that time has relentlessly passed, all his family are dead, and everything modern is cruel and terrible. Hearn spent the rest of his life trying to write his way back to that state of eternal dreaming, not by going back to Europe or the US, but by staying, and by way of chasing ghosts in things. He had a genius ability to *listen* to people and things — perhaps because he was partially blind, perhaps because he never could quite master the language — an ear that parsed the different music of a warbler and a cicada, the stamp of a peasant peddler and that of women in a summer festival. Perhaps that's why I like his single-topic essays best — on women's hair, an insect, a strange cave, the colour azure — because he focuses his intense attention not on vapour but on the distinctions of ordinary places and objects, and asks what kind of terror and superstitions — what whispering ghostliness — is woven in our everyday. Only after he moved to Tokyo ('Carpets — pianos — windows — curtains — brass bands — churches! How I hate them!! And white shirts!'), did he begin to listen for this kind of ghostliness, wrote Yone Noguchi — Hearn's counterpart in interpreting Japan for the West at the turn of the century — and only then 'did he begin to believe himself more Japanese than any other Japanese'. And that, Noguchi writes, is when Hearn's writing started getting *really* interesting.

But even Noguchi's observation — meant in appreciation of a man who had transmitted Japan's virtues to the Anglophone world — would've been unbearable to read had Setsu not been at Hearn's side, adjusting and checking the fit of his Japanese clothing, puncturing Hearn's own dreams about his 'Japanese-ness' at every turn. One time, she recounts, Hearn proclaimed that there was 'nothing Western about me'. To this she replied, 'You may have nothing Western about you, but look at your nose!' And he laughed, 'Oh! What can I do with my nose? Pity me because of this, for I, Koizumi Yakumo, truly love Japan more than any Japanese.' And what could he do — what can we do about own noses, the loves that we hold, despite, or perhaps because of, our blindnesses?

There's a photograph that is used as a cover-page of many of his biographies and his collected works. In it, he stands tall, looking sideways, a slight man in a sombre dark kimono and a hakama. I first instinctively rolled my eyes at it, until I realized with a shock that Hearn looks comfortable in his Japanese wear — it doesn't look like a costume, on him. The way that he carries his body in it held none of the peacocking, the hokey cosplay glee that usually accompanies a foreigner photographed in Japanese clothing. There is a quieter joy to it: Hearn looks like he was used to wearing something like it every day, which Setsu tells us he did, standing in his study, listening to the voice of locusts.

Lafcadio Hearn is buried in Zōshigaya Cemetery, Tokyo. Museums and other memorials are found in Lefkada, Tramore, New Orleans, Matsue, Kumamoto and Yaizu. Thank you for reading. Turn the page for the final image.

A men's kimono outfit, such as the one worn in this famous photograph of Lafcadio Hearn, tends to consist of five pieces including *hakama* trousers, *tabi* socks and a belt known as an *obi*.

LETTERS

Confused by Bulgarian booze, and let's all read more
theoretical texts.

Dear Happy Reader,

How amazing to receive issue 14 here in Bulgaria, and to see a small picture of Mastika Peshtera in the last essay! The brand is named after the village in Rodopa mountain where it's produced and where my family originally is from. It's where my grandfather once dreamed out loud about running from socialist Bulgaria, and his friend went straight to the militia. Grandfather was sent to a working camp for four years and the family left the town, but not forever — my uncle, a devoted mountaineer and a strange character, went back to build a small house in the hills far above Peshtera. I spent many a happy summer there as a kid and I still return often.

So it was a surprise even if I've never gotten near *mastika* in my life (the smell is... powerful). However I need to point out that *mastik* — which you wanted to illustrate as it was mentioned by Joris-Karl Huysmans — is another type of drink produced by a plant native to neighbouring Greece, *mastiha*; while what we call *mastika* is made from anise and is closer to ouzo. The actual *mastiha* liquor is a very different affair, being herbal, clean and somewhat volatile — it truly is as exquisite as it should be to fit our odd character of *Against Nature*.

Sevda Semer
Sofia, Bulgaria

Dear Happy Reader,

I wrote my university dissertation on Huysmans' *À Rebours*. For me, one of the most fascinating things about it is how it foreshadows Huysmans' embrace of Catholicism in later life. Strange as it might seem of such an ostentatiously 'decadent' and dyspeptically misanthropic book, it contains an intermittent yearning for some kind of spiritual antidote to the horror, stupidity and tedium which Huysmans' Des Esseintes see all around him. This is best expressed in the despairing (and beautiful) final sentence, in which Des Esseintes asks God to take pity on 'the galley-slave of life who puts out to sea alone in the night, beneath a firmament no longer lit by the consoling beacon-fires of the ancient hope'. Even if we don't share this desire for faith, the kind of existential angst Huysmans writes about feels — surprisingly perhaps for a book with a reputation like *À Rebours* — relatable.

All the best,
Ross Morran
Manchester, UK

Dear Happy Reader,

I was so pleased when Grace Wales Bonner said she read theoretical texts for pleasure. I feel so often that they are looked down as being too dense or boring, or something you read in college but rarely beyond. But I find so much enjoyment in them. They challenge my way of thinking and my perspective on literature, cultural ideologies, or both. They welcome a reader to an author's curiosity. In this way, they excite me and as Bonner puts it, "people can connect to a central idea and expand it. Expand what the world is..."

Warmest Regards,
Hailey Dezort
Chicago, Illinois

Experience the unparalleled pleasure of seeing your thoughts in print by sending an email, in response to anything in this issue, to letters@thehappyreader.com.

It's been a complicated year for *The Happy Reader* — as for everyone — which is why this issue is published in autumn as opposed to summer, and why it will be the only one this year. In 2021 *The Happy Reader* is scheduled to resume its usual summer-and-winter rhythm.

AN ADDICTIVE TRAGEDY

The Book of the Season for summer 2021, which we encourage you to read in advance of the issue so as to prepare for our next in-depth excavation, will be *Madonna in a Fur Coat*, a novel by Turkish writer Sabahattin Ali.

    Madonna in a Fur Coat is a melancholic love story that plays with traditional gender roles, and takes place during the interwar years in Berlin and Ankara. It was published in 1943 only to languish in obscurity for decades before suddenly becoming a runaway bestseller in recent years. But why? Is it that the conservative strictures at play in Turkey under the government of Recep Tayyip Erdoğan — a man seemingly preoccupied with old gender norms — have created a thirst for this subtly subversive work, by an author who was killed for his dissident views? Or is it that much of the world has acquired something of the illusory hedonism of interwar Berlin?

    Madonna in a Fur Coat, translated into English for the first time in 2016, is both a stone cold classic and a contemporary literary juggernaut.

SUBSCRIBE

    For over six years, *The Happy Reader* has been at once chronicling celebrated bookworms and magazinifying classic literature. Subscribe and never miss an issue by visiting boutiquemags.com.

    For the long months between this issue and the next, readers are encouraged to sign up for our popular fortnightly newsletter *Happy Readings* at thehappyreader.com/newsletter.

Jacket for *Madonna in a Fur Coat*, originally published in 1943.